Do not try to make George's Marvelous Medicine yourselves at home. It could be dangerous.

George is alone in the house with Grandma. The most horrid, grizzly old grunion of a grandma ever. She needs something stronger than her usual medicine to cure her grouchiness. A special grandma medicine, a remedy for *everything*. And George knows just what to put into it. Grandma's in for the surprise of her life—and so is George, when he sees the results of his mixture!

D0017732

Puffin Books by Roald Dahl

ROALD DAHL

GEORGE'S MARVELOUS MEDICINE

Illustrated by Quentin Blake

PUFFIN BOOKS

*This book is
for doctors everywhere*

PUFFIN BOOKS
An imprint of Penguin Random House LLC
375 Hudson Street
New York, New York 10014

First published in the United States of America by Alfred A. Knopf, Inc., 1982
Published by Puffin Books by arrangement with Alfred A. Knopf, Inc., 1991
Reissued in this edition by Puffin Books, an imprint of
Penguin Young Readers Group, 2007, 2013

THE LIBRARY OF CONGRESS HAS CATALOGED THE PREVIOUS PUFFIN BOOKS EDITION
UNDER CATALOG CARD NUMBER: 91-53034

Puffin Books ISBN 978-0-14-241035-6
Part of Boxed Set, ISBN 978-1-101-95044-9

Manufactured in China

3 5 7 9 10 8 6 4 2

Contents

Grandma

"**I'**m going shopping in the village," George's mother said to George on Saturday morning. "So be a good boy and don't get into mischief."

This was a silly thing to say to a small boy at any time. It immediately made him wonder what sort of mischief he might get into.

"And don't forget to give Grandma her medicine at eleven o'clock," the mother said. Then out she went, closing the back door behind her.

Grandma, who was dozing in her chair by the window, opened one wicked little eye and said, "Now you heard what your mother said, George. Don't forget my medicine."

"No, Grandma," George said.

"And just try to behave yourself for once while she's away."

"Yes, Grandma," George said.

George was bored to tears. He didn't have a brother or a sister. His father was a farmer, and the farm they lived on was miles away from anywhere, so there were never any children to play with. He was tired of staring at pigs and hens and cows and sheep. He was especially tired of having to live in the same house as that grizzly old grunion of a grandma. Looking after her all by himself was hardly the most exciting way to spend a Saturday morning.

"You can make me a nice cup of tea for a start," Grandma said to George. "That'll keep you out of mischief for a few minutes."

"Yes, Grandma," George said.

George couldn't help disliking Grandma. She was a selfish grumpy old woman. She had pale brown teeth and a small puckered-up mouth like a dog's bottom.

"How much sugar in your tea today, Grandma?" George asked her.

"One spoonful," she said. "And no milk."

Most grandmothers are lovely, kind, helpful old ladies, but not this one. She spent all day and every day sitting in her chair by the window, and she was always complaining, grousing, grouching, grumbling, griping about something or other. Never once, even on her best days, had she smiled at George and said, "Well, how are you this morning, George?" or, "Why don't you and I have a game of Snakes and Ladders?" or, "How was school today?" She didn't seem to care about other people, only about herself. She was a miserable old grouch.

George went into the kitchen and made Grandma a cup of tea with a teabag. He put one spoon of sugar in it and no milk. He stirred the sugar well and carried the cup into the living room.

Grandma sipped the tea. "It's not sweet enough," she said. "Put more sugar in."

George took the cup back to the kitchen and added another spoonful of sugar. He stirred it again and carried it carefully in to Grandma.

2

"Where's the saucer?" she said. "I won't have a cup without a saucer."

George fetched her a saucer.

"And what about a teaspoon, if you please?"

"I've stirred it for you, Grandma. I stirred it well."

"I'll stir my own tea, thank you very much," she said. "Fetch me a teaspoon."

George fetched her a teaspoon.

When George's mother or father was home, Grandma never ordered George about like this. It was only when she had him on her own that she began treating him badly.

"You know what's the matter with you?" the old woman said, staring at George over the rim of the teacup with those bright wicked little eyes. "You're *growing* too fast. Boys who grow too fast become stupid and lazy."

"But I can't help it if I'm growing fast, Grandma," George said.

"Of course you can," she snapped. "Growing's a nasty childish habit."

"But we *have* to grow, Grandma. If we didn't grow, we'd never be grown-ups."

"Rubbish, boy, rubbish," she said. "Look at me. Am I growing? Certainly not."

"But you did once, Grandma."

"Only *very little*," the old woman answered. "I gave up growing when I was extremely small, along with all the other nasty childish habits like laziness and disobedience and greed and sloppiness and untidiness and stupidity. You haven't given up any of these things, have you?"

"I'm still only a little boy, Grandma."

"You're eight years old," she snorted. "That's old enough to know better. If you don't stop growing soon, it'll be too late."

"Too late for what, Grandma?"

"It's ridiculous," she went on. "You're nearly as tall as me already."

George took a good look at Grandma. She certainly was a *very tiny* person. Her legs were so short she had to have a footstool to put her feet on, and her head only came halfway up the back of the armchair.

"Daddy says it's fine for a man to be tall," George said.

4

"Don't listen to your daddy," Grandma said. "Listen to me."

"But how do I stop myself growing?" George asked her.

"Eat less chocolate," Grandma said.

"Does chocolate make you grow?"

"It makes you grow the *wrong way*," she snapped. "Up instead of down."

Grandma sipped some tea but never took her eyes from the little boy who stood before her. "Never grow up," she said. "Always down."

"Yes, Grandma."

"And stop eating chocolate. Eat cabbage instead."

"Cabbage! Oh, no, I don't like cabbage," George said.

"It's not what you like or what you don't like," Grandma snapped. "It's what's good for you that counts. From now on, you must eat cabbage three times a day. Mountains of cabbage! And if it's got caterpillars in it, so much the better!"

"Ouch," George said.

"Caterpillars give you brains," the old woman said.

"Mummy washes them down the sink," George said.

"Mummy's as stupid as you are," Grandma said. "Cabbage doesn't taste of anything without a few boiled caterpillars in it. Slugs, too."

"Not *slugs!*" George cried out. "I couldn't eat slugs!"

"Whenever I see a live slug on a piece of lettuce," Grandma said, "I gobble it up quick before it crawls away. Delicious." She squeezed her lips together tight so that her mouth became a tiny wrinkled hole. "Delicious," she said again. "Worms and slugs and beetley bugs. You don't know what's good for you."

"You're joking, Grandma."

"I never joke," she said. "Beetles are perhaps best of all. They go *crunch!*"

"Grandma! That's beastly!"

The old hag grinned, showing those pale brown teeth. "Sometimes, if you're lucky," she said, "you get a beetle inside the stem of a stick of celery. That's what I like."

"Grandma! How *could* you?"

"You find all sorts of nice things in sticks of raw celery," the old woman went on. "Sometimes it's earwigs."

"I don't want to hear about it!" cried George.

"A big fat earwig is very tasty," Grandma said, licking her lips. "But you've got to be very quick, my dear, when you put one of those in your mouth. It has a pair of sharp nippers on its back end and if it grabs your tongue with those, it never lets go. So you've got to bite the earwig first, *chop chop*, before it bites you."

George started edging toward the door. He wanted to get as far away as possible from this filthy old woman.

"You're trying to get away from me, aren't you?" she said, pointing a finger straight at George's face. "You're trying to get away from Grandma."

Little George stood by the door staring at the old hag in the chair. She stared back at him.

Could it be, George wondered, that she was a witch? He had always thought witches were only in fairy tales, but now he was not so sure.

"Come closer to me, little boy," she said, beckoning to him with a horny finger. "Come closer to me and I will tell you *secrets*."

George didn't move.

Grandma didn't move either.

"I know a great many secrets," she said, and suddenly she smiled. It was a thin icy smile, the kind a snake might make just before it bites you. "Come over here to Grandma and she'll whisper secrets to you."

George took a step backward, edging closer to the door.

"You mustn't be frightened of your old grandma," she said, smiling that icy smile.

George took another step backward.

"Some of us," she said, and all at once she was leaning forward in her chair and whispering in a throaty sort of voice George had never heard her use before. "Some of us," she said, "have magic powers that can twist the creatures of this earth into wondrous shapes. . . ."

A tingle of electricity flashed down the length of George's spine. He began to feel frightened.

"Some of us," the old woman went on, "have fire on our tongues and sparks in our bellies and wizardry in the tips of our fingers. . . .

"Some of us know secrets that would make your hair stand straight up on end and your eyes pop out of their sockets. . . ."

George wanted to run away, but his feet seemed stuck to the floor.

"We know how to make your nails drop off and teeth grow out of your fingers instead."

George began to tremble. It was her face that frightened him most of all, the frosty smile, the brilliant unblinking eyes.

"We know how to have you wake up in the morning with a long tail coming out from behind you."

"Grandma!" he cried out. "Stop!"

"We know secrets, my dear, about dark places where dark things live and squirm and slither all over each other. . . ."

George made a dive for the door.

"It doesn't matter how far you run," he heard her saying, "you won't ever get away. . . ."

George ran into the kitchen, slamming the door behind him.

The Marvelous Plan

George sat himself down at the table in the kitchen. He was shaking a little. Oh, how he hated Grandma! He really *hated* that horrid old witchy woman. And all of a sudden he had a tremendous urge to *do something* about her. Something *whopping*. Something *absolutely terrific*. A *real shocker*. A sort of explosion. He wanted to blow away the witchy smell that hung about her in the next room. He may have been only eight years old, but he was a brave little boy. He was ready to take this old woman on.

"I'm not going to be frightened by *her*," he said softly to himself. But he *was* frightened. And that's why he wanted suddenly to explode her away.

Well . . . not quite away. But he did want to shake the old woman up a bit.

Very well, then. What should it be, this whopping terrific exploding shocker for Grandma?

He would have liked to put a firecracker under her chair, but he didn't have one.

He would have liked to put a long green snake down the back of her dress, but he didn't have a long green snake.

He would have liked to put six big black rats in the room with her and lock the door, but he didn't have six big black rats.

As George sat there pondering this interesting problem, his eye fell upon the bottle of Grandma's brown

medicine standing on the sideboard. Rotten stuff it seemed to be. Four times a day a large spoonful of it was shoveled into her mouth, and it didn't do her the slightest bit of good. She was always just as horrid after she'd had it as she'd been before. The whole point of medicine, surely, was to make a person better. If it didn't do that, then it was quite useless.

So-ho! thought George suddenly. *Ah-ha! Ho-hum!* I know exactly what I'll do. I shall make her a *new* medicine, one that is so strong and so fierce and so fantastic it will either cure her completely or blow off the top of her head. I'll make her a *magic medicine*, a medicine no doctor in the world has ever made before.

George looked at the kitchen clock. It said five past ten. There was nearly an hour left before Grandma's next dose was due at eleven.

"Here we go, then!" cried George, jumping up from the table. "A magic medicine it shall be!

"So give me a bug and a jumping flea,
Give me two snails and lizards three,
And a slimy squiggler from the sea,
And the poisonous sting of a bumblebee,
And the juice from the fruit of the jujube tree,
And the powdered bone of a wombat's knee.
And one hundred other things as well
Each with a rather nasty smell.
I'll stir them up, I'll boil them long,
A mixture tough, a mixture strong.
And then, heigh-ho, and down it goes,

12

A nice big spoonful (hold your nose)
Just gulp it down and have no fear.
'How do you like it, Granny dear?'
Will she go pop? Will she explode?
Will she go flying down the road?
Will she go poof in a puff of smoke?
Start fizzing like a can of Coke?
Who knows? Not I. Let's wait and see.
(I'm glad it's neither you nor me.)
Oh Grandma, if you only knew
What I have got in store for you!"

George Begins to Make the Medicine

George took an enormous stewing pot out of the cupboard and placed it on the kitchen table.

"George!" came the shrill voice from the next room. "What are you doing?"

"Nothing, Grandma," he called out.

"You needn't think I can't hear you just because you closed the door! You're rattling the pots and pans!"

"I'm just tidying the kitchen, Grandma."

Then there was silence.

George had absolutely no doubts whatsoever about how he was going to make his famous medicine. He wasn't going to fool about wondering whether to put in a little bit of this or a little bit of that. Quite simply, he was going to put in EVERYTHING he could find. There would be no messing about, no hesitating, no wondering whether a particular thing would knock the old girl sideways or not. The rule would be this: Whatever he saw, if it was runny or powdery or gooey, in it went.

Nobody had ever made a medicine like that before. If it didn't actually cure Grandma, then it would anyway cause some exciting results. It would be worth watching.

George decided to work his way around the various rooms one at a time and see what they had to offer.

He would go first to the bathroom. There are always lots of funny things in a bathroom. So upstairs he

14

went, carrying the enormous two-handled pot before him.

In the bathroom, he gazed longingly at the famous and dreaded medicine cupboard. But he didn't go near it. It was the only thing in the entire house he was forbidden to touch. He had made solemn promises to his parents about this, and he wasn't going to break them. There were things in there, they had told him, that could actually kill a person, and although he was out to give Grandma a pretty fiery mouthful, he didn't really want a dead body on his hands. George put the stewpot on the floor and went to work.

Number one was a bottle labeled GOLDENGLOSS HAIR SHAMPOO. He emptied it into the pot. "That ought to wash her tummy nice and clean," he said.

He took a full tube of TOOTHPASTE and squeezed out the whole lot of it in one long worm. "Maybe that will brighten up those horrid brown teeth of hers," he said.

There was an aerosol can of SUPERFOAM SHAVING SOAP belonging to his father. George loved playing with aerosols. He pressed the button and kept his finger on it until there was nothing left. A wonderful mountain of white foam built up in the giant pot.

With his fingers, he scooped out the contents of a jar of VITAMIN ENRICHED FACE CREAM.

In went a small bottle of scarlet NAIL POLISH. "If the toothpaste doesn't clean her teeth," George said, "then this will paint them as red as roses."

He found another jar of creamy stuff labeled HAIR REMOVER. SMEAR IT ON YOUR LEGS, it said, AND ALLOW TO REMAIN FOR FIVE MINUTES. George tipped it all into the pot.

There was a bottle with yellow stuff inside it called DISHWORTH'S FAMOUS DANDRUFF CURE. In it went.

There was something called BRILLIDENT FOR CLEANING FALSE TEETH. It was a white powder. In that went, too.

He found another aerosol can, NEVERMORE PONGING DEODORANT SPRAY, GUARANTEED, it said, TO KEEP AWAY UNPLEASANT BODY SMELLS FOR A WHOLE DAY. "She could use plenty of that," George said as he sprayed the entire canful into the stewing pot.

LIQUID PARAFFIN, the next one was called. It was a big bottle. He hadn't the faintest idea what it did to you, but he poured it in anyway.

That, he thought, looking around him, was about all from the bathroom.

On his mother's dressing table in the bedroom George found yet another lovely aerosol can. It was called HELGA'S HAIRSET. HOLD TWELVE INCHES AWAY FROM THE HAIR AND SPRAY LIGHTLY. He squirted the whole lot into the pot. He *did* enjoy squirting these aerosols.

There was a bottle of perfume called FLOWERS OF TURNIPS. It smelled of old cheese. In it went.

And in, too, went a large round box of POWDER that was called PINK PLASTER. There was a powder puff on top, and he threw that in as well for luck.

He found a couple of LIPSTICKS. He pulled the greasy red things out of their little cases and added them to the mixture.

The bedroom had nothing more to offer, so George carried the enormous pot downstairs again and trotted into the laundry room where the shelves were full of all kinds of household items.

The first one he took down was a large box of SUPERWHITE FOR AUTOMATIC WASHING MACHINES. DIRT, it said, WILL DISAPPEAR LIKE MAGIC. George didn't know whether Grandma was automatic or not, but she was certainly a dirty old woman. "So she'd better have it all," he said, tipping in the whole boxful.

Then there was a big can of WAXWELL FLOOR POLISH. IT REMOVES FILTH AND FOUL MESSES FROM YOUR FLOOR AND LEAVES EVERYTHING SHINY BRIGHT, it said. George scooped the orange-colored waxy stuff out of the can and plunked it into the pot.

There was a round cardboard carton labeled FLEA POWDER FOR DOGS. KEEP WELL AWAY FROM THE DOG'S FOOD, it said, BECAUSE THIS POWDER, IF EATEN, WILL MAKE THE DOG EXPLODE. "Good," said George, pouring it all into the stewing pot.

He found a box of CANARY SEED on the shelf. "Perhaps it'll make the old bird sing," he said, and in it went.

Next, George explored the box with shoe-cleaning materials—brushes and cans and polishing cloths. Well now, he thought, Grandma's medicine is brown, so *my* medicine must also be brown, or she'll smell a rat. The way to color it, he decided, would be with BROWN SHOE POLISH. The large can he chose was labeled DARK TAN. Splendid. He scooped it all out with an old spoon and plopped it into the pot. He would stir it up later.

On his way back to the kitchen, George saw a bottle of GIN standing on the sideboard. Grandma was very fond of gin. She was allowed to have a small nip of it every evening. Now he would give her a treat. He would pour in the whole bottle. He did.

Back in the kitchen, George put the huge stewing pot on the table and went over to the cupboard that served as a larder. The shelves were bulging with bottles and jars of every sort. He chose the following and emptied them one by one into the pot:

A TIN OF CURRY POWDER

A TIN OF MUSTARD POWDER

A BOTTLE OF "EXTRA HOT" CHILI SAUCE

A TIN OF BLACK PEPPERCORNS

A BOTTLE OF HORSERADISH SAUCE

"There!" he said aloud. "That should do it!"

"George!" came the screechy voice from the next room. "Who are you talking to in there? What are you up to?"

"Nothing, Grandma, absolutely nothing," he called back.

"Is it time for my medicine yet?"

"No, Grandma, not for about half an hour."

"Well, just see you don't forget it."

"I won't, Grandma," George answered. "I promise I won't."

Animal Pills

At this point, George suddenly had an extra good wheeze. Although the medicine cupboard in the house was forbidden ground, what about the medicines his father kept on the shelf in the shed next to the henhouse? The animal medicines?

What about *those*?

Nobody had ever told him he mustn't touch *them*.

Let's face it, George said to himself, hair spray and shaving cream and shoe polish are all very well, and they will no doubt cause some splendid explosions inside the old geezer, but what the magic mixture now needs is a touch of the real stuff, real pills and real tonics, to give it punch and muscle.

George picked up the heavy three-quarters full pot and carried it out the back door. He crossed the farmyard and headed straight for the shed alongside the henhouse. He knew his father wouldn't be there. He was out haymaking in one of the meadows.

George entered the dusty old shed and put the stewing pot on the bench. Then he looked up at the medicine shelf. There were five big bottles there. Two were full of pills, two were full of runny stuff and one was full of powder.

"I'll use them all," George said. "Grandma needs them. Boy, does she need them!"

The first bottle he took down contained an orange-colored powder. The label said, FOR CHICKENS WITH

FOUL PEST, HEN GRIPE, SORE BEAKS, GAMMY LEGS,
COCKERELITIS, EGG TROUBLE, BROODINESS OR LOSS OF
FEATHERS. MIX ONE SPOONFUL ONLY WITH EACH BUCKET
OF FEED.

"Well," George said aloud to himself as he tipped in
the whole bottleful, "the old bird won't be losing any
feathers after she's had a dose of this."

The next bottle he took down had about five hundred gigantic purple pills in it. FOR HORSES WITH

HOARSE THROATS, it said on the label. THE HOARSE-THROATED HORSE SHOULD SUCK ONE PILL TWICE A DAY.

"Grandma may not have a hoarse throat," George said, "but she's certainly got a sharp tongue. Maybe they'll cure that instead." Into the pot went the five hundred gigantic purple pills.

Then there was a bottle of thick yellowish liquid. FOR COWS, BULLS AND BULLOCKS, the label said. WILL CURE COWPOX, COW MANGE, CRUMPLED HORNS, BAD BREATH IN BULLS, EARACHE, TOOTHACHE, HEADACHE, HOOFACHE, TAILACHE AND SORE UDDERS.

"That grumpy old cow in the living room has every one of those rotten illnesses," George said. "She'll need it all." With a slop and a gurgle, the yellow liquid splashed into the now nearly full stewpot.

The next bottle contained a brilliant red liquid. SHEEPDIP, it said on the label. FOR SHEEP WITH SHEEP ROT AND FOR GETTING RID OF TICKS AND FLEAS. MIX ONE SPOONFUL IN ONE GALLON OF WATER AND SLOSH IT OVER

THE SHEEP. CAUTION, DO NOT MAKE THE MIXTURE ANY STRONGER OR THE WOOL WILL FALL OUT AND THE ANIMAL WILL BE NAKED.

"By gum," said George, "how I'd love to walk in and slosh it all over old Grandma and watch the ticks and fleas go jumping off her. But I can't. I mustn't. So she'll have to drink it instead." He poured the bright red medicine into the pot.

The last bottle on the shelf was full of pale green pills. PIG PILLS, the label announced. FOR PIGS WITH PORK PRICKLES, TENDER TROTTERS, BRISTLE BLIGHT AND SWINE SICKNESS. GIVE ONE PILL PER DAY. IN SEVERE CASES TWO PILLS MAY BE GIVEN, BUT MORE THAN THAT WILL MAKE THE PIG ROCK AND ROLL.

"Just the stuff," said George, "for that miserable old pig back there in the house. She'll need a very big dose." He tipped all the green pills, hundreds and hundreds of them, into the stewing pot.

There was an old stick lying on the bench that had been used for stirring paint. George picked it up and started to stir his marvelous concoction. The mixture was as thick as cream, and as he stirred and stirred, many wonderful colors rose up from the depths and blended together, pinks, blues, greens, yellows and browns.

George went on stirring until it was all well mixed, but even so there were still hundreds of pills lying on the bottom that hadn't melted. And there was his mother's splendid powder puff floating on the surface. "I shall have to boil it all," George said. "One good quick boil on the stove is all it needs." And with that

25

he staggered back toward the house with the enormous heavy stewing pot.

On the way, he passed the garage, so he went in to see if he could find any other interesting things. He added the following:

Half a pint of ENGINE OIL—to keep Grandma's engine going smoothly.

Some ANTIFREEZE—to keep her radiator from freezing up in winter.

A handful of GREASE—to grease her creaking joints.

Then back to the kitchen.

The Cook-up

In the kitchen, George put the heavy stewing pot on the stove and turned up the gas flame underneath it as high as it would go.

"George!" came the awful voice from the next room. "It's time for my medicine!"

"Not yet, Grandma," George called back. "There's still twenty minutes before eleven o'clock."

"What mischief are you up to in there now?" Granny screeched. "I hear noises."

George thought it best not to answer this one. He found a long wooden spoon in a kitchen drawer and began stirring hard. The stuff in the pot got hotter and hotter.

Soon the marvelous mixture began to froth and foam. A rich blue smoke, the color of peacocks, rose from the surface of the liquid, and a fiery fearsome smell filled the kitchen. It made George choke and splutter. It was a smell unlike any he had smelled before. It was a brutal and bewitching smell, spicy and staggering, fierce and frenzied, full of wizardry and magic. Whenever he got a whiff of it up his nose, fire-crackers went off in his skull and electric prickles ran along the backs of his legs. It was wonderful to stand there stirring this amazing mixture and to watch it smoking blue and bubbling and frothing and foaming as though it were alive. At one point, he could have sworn he saw bright sparks flashing in the swirling foam.

And suddenly George found himself dancing around the steaming pot, chanting strange words that came into his head out of nowhere:

> "Fiery broth and witch's brew
> Foamy froth and riches blue
> Fume and spume and spoondrift spray
> Fizzle swizzle shout hooray
> Watch it sloshing, swashing, sploshing
> Hear it hissing, squishing, spissing
> Grandma better start to pray."

Brown Paint

George turned off the heat under the stewing pot. He must leave plenty of time for it to cool down.

When all the steam and froth had gone away, he peered into the giant pot to see what color the great medicine now was. It was a deep and brilliant blue.

"It needs more brown in it," George said. "It simply must be brown, or she'll get suspicious."

George ran outside and dashed into his father's toolshed where all the paints were kept. There was a row of cans on the shelf, all colors, black, green, red, pink, white and brown. He reached for the can of brown. The label said simply DARK BROWN GLOSS PAINT ONE QUART. He took a screwdriver and prised off the lid. The can was three-quarters full. He rushed it back to the kitchen. He poured the whole lot into the pot. The pot was now full to the brim. Very gently, George stirred the paint into the mixture with the long wooden spoon. *Ah-ha!* It was all turning brown! A lovely rich creamy brown!

"Where's that medicine of mine, boy?!" came the voice from the living room. "You're forgetting me! You're doing it on purpose! I shall tell your mother!"

"I'm not forgetting you, Grandma," George called back. "I'm thinking of you all the time. But there are still ten minutes to go."

"You're a nasty little maggot!" The voice screeched

29

back. "You're a lazy and disobedient little worm and you're growing too fast."

George fetched the bottle of Grandma's real medicine from the sideboard. He took out the cork and tipped it all down the sink. He then filled the bottle with his own magic mixture by dipping a small jug into the pot and using it as a pourer. He replaced the cork.

Had it cooled down enough yet? Not quite. He held the bottle under the cold tap for a couple of minutes. The label came off in the water, but that didn't matter. He dried the bottle with a dishcloth.

All was now ready!

This was it!

The great moment had arrived!

"Medicine time, Grandma!" he called out.

"I should hope so, too," came the grumpy reply.

The silver tablespoon in which the medicine was always given lay ready on the kitchen sideboard. George picked it up.

Holding the spoon in one hand and the bottle in the other, he advanced into the living room.

Grandma Gets the Medicine

Grandma sat hunched in her chair by the window. The wicked little eyes followed George closely as he crossed the room toward her.

"You're late," she snapped.

"I don't think I am, Grandma."

"Don't interrupt me in the middle of a sentence!" she shouted.

"But you'd finished your sentence, Grandma."

"There you go again!" she cried. "Always interrupting and arguing. You really are a tiresome little boy. What's the time?"

"It's exactly eleven o'clock, Grandma."

"You're lying as usual. Stop talking so much and give me my medicine. Shake the bottle first. Then pour it onto the spoon and make sure it's a whole spoonful."

"Are you going to gulp it all down in one go?" George asked her. "Or will you sip it?"

"What I do is none of your business," the old woman said. "Fill the spoon."

As George removed the cork and began very slowly to pour the thick brown stuff into the spoon, he couldn't help thinking back on all the mad and marvelous things that had gone into the making of this crazy stuff—the shaving soap, the hair remover, the dandruff cure, the automatic washing-machine powder, the flea powder for dogs, the shoe polish, the black pepper, the horseradish sauce and all the rest of them, not to mention the powerful animal pills and powders and liquids . . . and the brown paint.

"Open your mouth wide, Grandma," he said, "and I'll pop it in."

The old hag opened her small wrinkled mouth, showing disgusting pale brown teeth.

"Here we go!" George cried out. "Swallow it down!" He pushed the spoon well into her mouth and tipped the mixture down her throat. Then he stepped back to watch the result.

It was worth watching.

Grandma yelled *"Oweeeee!"* and her whole body shot up *whoosh* into the air. It was exactly as though someone had pushed an electric wire through the underneath of her chair and switched on the current. Up she went like a jack-in-the-box . . . and she didn't come down . . . she stayed there . . . suspended in midair . . . about two feet up . . . still in a sitting position . . . but rigid now . . . frozen . . . quivering . . . the eyes bulging . . . the hair standing straight up on end.

"Is something wrong, Grandma?" George asked her politely. "Are you all right?"

Suspended up there in space, the old girl was beyond speaking.

The shock that George's marvelous mixture had given her must have been tremendous.

You'd have thought she'd swallowed a red-hot poker the way she took off from that chair.

Then down she came again with a *plop*, back into her seat.

"Call the fire department!" she shouted suddenly.
"My stomach's on fire!"

"It's just the medicine, Grandma," George said.
"It's good strong stuff."

"Fire!" the old woman yelled. "Fire in the basement!
Get a bucket! Man the hoses! Do something quick!"

"Cool it, Grandma," George said. But he got a bit of
a shock when he saw the smoke coming out of her
mouth and out of her nostrils. Clouds of black smoke
were coming out of her nose and blowing around the
room.

"By golly, you really are on fire," George said.

"Of course I'm on fire!" she yelled. "I'll be burned to a crisp! I'll be fried to a frizzle! I'll be boiled like a beetroot!"

George ran into the kitchen and came back with a jug of water. "Open your mouth, Grandma!" he cried. He could hardly see her for the smoke, but he managed to pour half a jugful down her throat. A sizzling sound, the kind you get if you hold a hot frying pan under cold water, came up from deep down in Grandma's stomach. The old hag bucked and shied and snorted. She gasped and gurgled. Spouts of water came shooting out of her. And the smoke cleared away.

"The fire's out," George announced proudly. "You'll be all right now, Grandma."

"*All right?*" she yelled. "Who's *all right?* There's jacky-jumpers in my tummy! There's squigglers in my belly! There's bangers in my bottom!" She began bouncing up and down in the chair. Quite obviously, she was not very comfortable.

"You'll find it's doing you a lot of good, that medicine, Grandma," George said.

"*Good?*" she screamed. "Doing me *good?* It's *killing* me!"

Then she began to bulge.

She was swelling.

She was puffing up all over!

Someone was pumping her up, that's how it looked!

Was she going to explode?

Her face was turning from purple to green!

34

But wait! She had a puncture somewhere! George could hear the hiss of escaping air. She stopped swelling. She was going down. She was slowly getting thinner again, shrinking back and back slowly to her shrivelly old self.

"How's things, Grandma?" George said.

No answer.

Then a funny thing happened. Grandma's body gave a sudden sharp twist and a sudden sharp jerk and she flipped herself clear out of the chair and landed neatly on her two feet on the carpet.

"That's terrific, Grandma!" George cried. "You haven't stood up like that for years! Look at you! You're standing up all on your own and you're not even using a stick!"

Grandma didn't even hear him. The frozen pop-eyed look was back with her again now. She was miles away in another world.

Marvelous medicine, George told himself. He found it fascinating to stand there watching what it was doing to the old hag. What next? he wondered.

He soon found out.

Suddenly she began to grow.

It was quite slow at first . . . just a very gradual inching upward . . . up, up, up . . . inch by inch . . . getting taller and taller . . . about an inch every few seconds . . . and in the beginning George didn't notice it.

But when she had passed the five-foot-six mark and was going on up toward being six feet tall, George gave a jump and shouted, "Hey, Grandma! You're *growing!* You're *going up!* Hang on, Grandma! You'd better stop now or you'll be hitting the ceiling!"

But Grandma didn't stop.

It was a truly fantastic sight, this ancient scrawny old woman getting taller and taller, longer and longer,

36

thinner and thinner, as though she were a piece of elastic being pulled upward by invisible hands.

When the top of her head actually touched the ceiling, George thought she was bound to stop.

But she didn't.

There was a sort of scrunching noise, and bits of plaster and cement came raining down.

"Hadn't you better stop now, Grandma?" George said. "Daddy's just had this whole room repainted."

But there was no stopping her now.

Soon, her head and shoulders had completely disappeared through the ceiling, and she was still going.

George dashed upstairs to his own bedroom, and there she was, coming up through the floor like a mushroom.

"Whoopee!" she shouted, finding her voice at last. "Hallelujah, here I come!"

"Steady, Grandma," George said.

"With a heigh-nonny-no and up we go!" she shouted. "Just watch me grow!"

"This is *my* room," George said. "Look at the mess you're making."

"Terrific medicine!" she cried. "Give me some more!"

She's dotty as a doughnut, George thought.

"Come on, boy! Give me some more!" she yelled. "Dish it out! I'm slowing down!"

George was still clutching the medicine bottle in one

hand and the spoon in the other. Oh well, he thought, why not? He poured out a second dose and popped it into her mouth.

"*Oweee!*" she screamed, and up she went again. Her feet were still on the floor downstairs in the living room, but her head was moving quickly toward the ceiling of the bedroom.

"I'm on my way now, boy!" she called down to George. "Just watch me go!"

"That's the attic above you, Grandma!" George called out. "I'd keep out of there! It's full of bugs and bogles!"

Crash! The old girl's head went through the ceiling as though it were butter.

George stood in his bedroom gazing at the shambles. There was a big hole in the floor and another in the ceiling, and sticking up like a post between the two was the middle part of Grandma. Her legs were in the room below, her head in the attic.

"I'm still going!" came the old screechy voice from up above. "Give me another dose, my boy, and let's go through the roof!"

"No, Grandma, no!" George called back. "You're busting up the whole house!"

"To heck with the house!" she shouted. "I want some fresh air! I haven't been outside for twenty years!"

"By golly, she *is* going through the roof!" George told himself. He ran downstairs. He rushed out the back door into the yard. It would be simply awful, he thought, if she bashed up the roof as well. His father would be furious. And he, George, would get the blame. *He* had made the medicine. *He* had given her too much. "Don't come through the roof, Grandma," he prayed. "Please don't."

The Brown Hen

George stood in the farmyard looking up at the roof. The old farmhouse had a fine roof of pale red tiles and tall chimneys.

There was no sign of Grandma. There was only a song thrush sitting on one of the chimney pots, singing a song. The old wurzel's got stuck in the attic, George thought. Thank goodness for that.

Suddenly a tile came clattering down from the roof and fell into the yard. The thrush took off fast and flew away.

Then another tile came down.

Then half a dozen more.

And then, very slowly, like some weird monster rising up from the deep, Grandma's head came through the roof. . . .

Then her scrawny neck. . . .

And the tops of her shoulders. . . .

"How'm I doing, boy!" she shouted. "How's that for a bash up?"

"Don't you think you'd better stop now, Grandma?" George called out.

"I have stopped!" she answered. "I feel terrific! Didn't I tell you I had magic powers! Didn't I warn you I had wizardry in the tips of my fingers! But you wouldn't listen to me, would you? You wouldn't listen to your old Grandma!"

"*You* didn't do it, Grandma," George shouted back

to her. "*I* did it! I made you a new medicine!"

"A *new medicine? You?* What rubbish!" she yelled.

"I did! I did!" George shouted.

"You're lying as usual!" Grandma yelled. "You're always lying!"

"I'm not lying, Grandma. I swear I'm not."

The wrinkled old face high up on the roof stared down suspiciously at George. "Are you telling me you actually made a new medicine all by yourself?" she shouted.

"Yes, Grandma, all by myself."

"I don't believe you," she answered. "But I'm very comfortable up here. Fetch me a cup of tea."

A brown hen was pecking about in the yard close to where George was standing. The hen gave him an idea. Quickly, he uncorked the medicine bottle and poured some of the brown stuff into the spoon. "Watch this, Grandma!" he shouted. He crouched down, holding out the spoon to the hen.

"Chicken," he said. "Chick-chick-chicken. Come here. Have some of this."

Chickens are stupid birds, and very greedy. They think everything is food. This one thought the spoon was full of corn. It hopped over. It put its head on one side and looked at the spoon. "Come on, chicken," George said. "Good chicken. Chick-chick-chick."

The brown hen stretched out its neck toward the spoon and went *peck*. It got a beakful of medicine.

The effect was electric.

"*Oweee!*" shrieked the hen and it shot straight up into the air like a rocket. It went as high as the house.

Then down it came again into the yard, *splosh*. And there it sat with its feathers all sticking straight out from its body. There was a look of amazement on its silly face. George stood watching it. Grandma up on the roof was watching it, too.

The hen got to its feet. It was rather shaky. It was making funny gurgling noises in its throat. Its beak was opening and shutting. It seemed like a pretty sick hen.

"You've done it in, you stupid boy!" Grandma shouted. "That hen's going to die! Your father'll be after you now! He'll give you socks and serve you right!"

All of a sudden, black smoke started pouring out of the hen's beak.

"It's on fire!" Grandma yelled. "The hen's on fire!"

George ran to the water trough to get a bucket of water.

"That hen'll be roasted and ready for eating any moment!" Grandma shouted.

George sloshed the bucket of water over the hen. There was a sizzling sound, and the smoke went away.

"Old hen's laid its last egg!" Grandma shouted. "Hens don't do any laying after they've been on fire!"

Now that the fire was out, the hen seemed better. It stood up properly. It flapped its wings. Then it crouched down low to the ground, as though getting ready to jump. It did jump. It jumped high in the air and turned a complete somersault, then landed back on its feet.

"It's a circus hen!" Grandma shouted from the rooftop. "It's a flipping acrobat!"

Now the hen began to grow.

45

George had been waiting for this to happen. "It's growing!" he yelled. "It's growing, Grandma! Look, it's growing!"

Bigger and bigger . . . taller and taller it grew. Soon the hen was four or five times its normal size.

"Can you see it, Grandma?" George shouted.

"I can see it, boy!" the old woman shouted back. "I'm watching it!"

George was hopping about from one foot to the other with excitement, pointing at the enormous hen and shouting, "It's had the magic medicine, Grandma, and it's growing just like you did!"

But there was a difference between the way the hen was growing and the way Grandma grew. When Grandma grew taller and taller, she got thinner and thinner. The hen didn't. It stayed nice and plump all along.

Soon it was taller than George, but it didn't stop there. It went right on growing until it was about as big as a horse. Then it stopped.

"Doesn't it look marvelous, Grandma!" George shouted.

"It's not as tall as me!" Grandma sang out. "Compared with me, that hen is titchy small! I am the tallest of them all!"

The Pig, the Bullocks, the Sheep, the Pony and the Nanny Goat

At that moment, George's mother came back from shopping in the village. She drove her car into the yard and got out. She was carrying a bottle of milk in one hand and a bag of groceries in the other.

The first thing she saw was the gigantic brown hen towering over little George. She dropped the bottle of milk.

Then Grandma started shouting at her from the rooftop, and when she looked up and saw Grandma's head sticking up through the tiles, she dropped the bag of groceries.

"How about that then, eh, Mary?" Grandma shouted. "I'll bet you've never seen a hen as big as that! That's George's giant hen, that is!"

"But . . . but . . . but . . ." stammered George's mother.

"It's George's magic medicine!" Grandma shouted. "We've both of us had it, the hen and I!"

"But how in the world did you get up on the roof?" cried the mother.

"I didn't!" cackled the old woman. "My feet are still standing on the floor in the living room!"

This was too much for George's mother to understand. She just goggled and gaped. She looked as though she was going to faint.

A second later, George's father appeared. His name was Mr. Killy Kranky. Mr. Kranky was a small man

48

with bandy legs and a huge head. He was a kind father to George, but he was not an easy person to live with because even the smallest things got him all worked up and excited. The hen standing in the yard was certainly not a small thing, and when Mr. Kranky saw it, he started jumping about as though something was burning his feet. "Great heavens!" he cried, waving his arms. "What's this? What's happened? Where did it come from? It's a giant hen! Who did it?"

"I did," George said.

"Look at *me*!" Grandma shouted from the rooftop. "Never mind about the hen! What about *me*?"

Mr. Kranky looked up and saw Grandma. "Shut up, Grandma," he said. It didn't seem to surprise him that the old girl was sticking up through the roof. It was the hen that excited him. He had never seen anything like it. But then who had?

"It's fantastic!" Mr. Kranky shouted, dancing around and around. "It's colossal! It's gigantic! It's tremendous! It's a miracle! How did you do it, George?"

George started telling his father about the magic medicine. While he was doing this, the big brown hen sat down in the middle of the yard and went *cluck-cluck-cluck . . . cluck-cluck-cluck-cluck-cluck*.

Everyone stared at it.

When it stood up again, there was a brown egg lying there. The egg was the size of a football.

"That egg would make scrambled eggs for twenty people!" Mrs. Kranky said.

"George!" Mr. Kranky shouted. "How much of this medicine have you got?"

"Lots," George said. "There's a big potful in the kitchen, and this bottle here's nearly full."

"Come with me!" Mr. Kranky yelled, grabbing George by the arm. "Bring the medicine! For years and years I've been trying to breed bigger and bigger animals. Bigger bulls for beef. Bigger pigs for pork. Bigger sheep for mutton. . . ."

They went to the pigsty first.

George gave a spoonful of the medicine to the pig.

The pig blew smoke from its nose and jumped about all over the place. Then it grew and grew.

In the end, it looked like this. . . .

They went to the herd of fine black bullocks that
Mr. Kranky was trying to fatten for the market.

George gave each of them some medicine, and this is what happened. . . .

Then the sheep. . . .

He gave some to his gray pony, Jack Frost. . . .

And finally, just for fun, he gave some to Alma, the nanny goat. . . .

A Crane for Grandma

Grandma, from high up on the rooftop, could see everything that was going on, and she didn't like what she saw. She wanted to be the center of attention, and nobody was taking the slightest notice of her. George and Mr. Kranky were running around and getting excited about the enormous animals. Mrs. Kranky was washing up in the kitchen, and Grandma was all alone on the rooftop.

"Hey you!" she yelled. "George! Get me a cup of tea this minute, you idle little beast!"

"Don't listen to the old goat," Mr. Kranky said. "She's stuck where she is, and a good thing, too."

"But we can't leave her up there, Dad," George said. "What if it rains?"

"George!" Grandma yelled. "Oh, you horrible little boy! You disgusting little worm! Fetch me a cup of tea at once and a slice of currant cake!"

"We'll have to get her out, Dad," George said. "She won't give us any peace if we don't."

Mrs. Kranky came outside, and she agreed with George. "She's my own mother," she said.

"She's a pain in the neck," Mr. Kranky said.

"I don't care," Mrs. Kranky said. "I'm not leaving my own mother sticking up through the roof for the rest of her life."

So in the end, Mr. Kranky telephoned the Crane Company and asked them to send their biggest crane out to the house at once.

The crane arrived one hour later. It was on wheels, and there were two men inside it. The crane men climbed up onto the roof and put ropes under Grandma's arms. Then she was lifted right up through the roof. . . .

In a way, the medicine had done Grandma good. It had not made her any less grumpy or bad-tempered, but it seemed to have cured all her aches and pains, and she was suddenly as frisky as a ferret. As soon as the crane had lowered her to the ground, she ran over to George's huge pony, Jack Frost, and jumped onto his back. This ancient old hag, who was now as tall as a house, then galloped about the farm on the gigantic pony, jumping over trees and sheds and shouting, "Out of my way! Clear the decks! Stand back all you miserable midgets or I'll trample you to death!" and other silly things like that.

But because Grandma was now much too tall to get back into the house, she had to sleep that night in the hay barn with the mice and the rats.

Mr. Kranky's Great Idea

The next day, George's father came down to breakfast in a state of greater excitement than ever. "I've been awake all night thinking about it!" he cried.

"About what, Dad?" George asked him.

"About your marvelous medicine, of course! We can't stop now, my boy! We must start making more of it at once! More and more and more!"

The giant stewing pot had been completely emptied the day before because there had been so many sheep and pigs and cows and bullocks to be dosed.

"But why do we need more, Dad?" George asked. "We've done all our own animals, and we've made Grandma feel as frisky as a ferret, even though she does have to to sleep in the barn."

"My dear boy," cried Mr. Killy Kranky, "we need barrels and barrels of it! Tons and tons! Then we will sell it to every farmer in the world so that all of them can have giant animals! We will build a Marvelous Medicine Factory and sell the stuff in bottles at ten dollars apiece. We will become rich, and you will become famous!"

"But wait a minute, Dad," George said.

"There's no waiting!" cried Mr. Kranky, working himself up so much that he put butter in his coffee and milk on his toast. "Don't you understand what this tremendous invention of yours is going to do to the world? Nobody will ever go hungry again!"

"Why won't they?" asked George.

"Because one giant cow will give fifty buckets of milk a day!" cried Mr. Kranky, waving his arms. "One giant chicken will make a hundred fried chicken dinners, and one giant pig will give you a thousand pork chops! It's tremendous, my dear boy! It's fantastic! It'll change the world."

"But wait a minute, Dad," George said again.

"Don't keep saying wait a minute!" shouted Mr. Kranky. "There isn't a minute to *wait!* We must get cracking at once!"

"Do calm down, my dear," Mrs. Kranky said from the other end of the table. "And stop putting marmalade on your cornflakes."

"The heck with my cornflakes!" cried Mr. Kranky, leaping up from his chair. "Come on, George! Let's get going! And the first thing we'll do is to make one more stewpotful as a tester."

"But, Dad," said little George. "The trouble is . . ."

"There won't be any trouble, my boy!" cried Mr. Kranky. "How can there possibly be any trouble? All you've got to do is put the same stuff into the pot as you did yesterday. And while you're doing it, I'll write down each and every item. That's how we'll get the magic recipe!"

"But, Dad," George said. "Please listen to me."

"Why don't you listen to him?" Mrs. Kranky said. "The boy's trying to tell you something."

But Mr. Kranky was too excited to listen to anyone except himself. "And then," he cried, "when the new mixture is ready, we'll test it out on an old hen just to make sure we've got it right, and after that we'll all shout hooray and build the giant factory!"

"But, Dad . . ."

"Come on then, what is it you want to say?"

"I can't possibly remember all the hundreds of things I put into the pot to make the medicine," George said.

"Of course you can, my dear boy," cried Mr. Kranky. "I'll help you! I'll jog your memory! You'll get it in the end, you see if you don't! Now then, what was the very first thing you put in?"

"I went up to the bathroom first," George said. "I used a lot of things in the bathroom and on mummy's dressing table."

"Come on, then!" cried Mr. Kranky. "Up we go to the bathroom!"

When they got there, they found, of course, a whole lot of empty tubes and empty aerosol cans and empty bottles. "That's great," said Mr. Kranky. "That tells us exactly what you used. If anything is empty, it means you used it."

So Mr. Kranky started making a list of everything that was empty in the bathroom. Then they went to Mrs. Kranky's dressing table. "A box of powder," said Mr. Kranky, writing it down. "Helga's Hair Set. Flowers of Turnips perfume. Terrific. This is going to be easy. Where did you go next?"

"To the laundry room," George said. "But are you sure you haven't missed anything up here, Dad?"

"That's up to you, my boy," Mr. Kranky said. "Have I?"

"I don't think so," George said. So down they went to the laundry room, and once again Mr. Kranky wrote down the names of all the empty bottles and cans. "My goodness me, what a mass of stuff you used!" he cried. "No wonder it did magic things! Is that the lot?"

"No, Dad, it's not," George said, and he led his father out to the shed where the animal medicines were kept and showed him the five big empty bottles up on the shelf. Mr. Kranky wrote down all their names.

"Anything else?" Mr. Kranky asked.

Little George scratched his head and thought and thought, but he couldn't remember having put anything else in.

Mr. Killy Kranky leapt into his car and drove down to the village and bought new bottles and tubes and cans of everything on his list. He then went to the vet and got a fresh supply of all the animal medicines George had used.

"Now show me how you did it, George," he said. "Come along. Show me exactly how you mixed them all together."

Marvelous Medicine Number Two

They were in the kitchen now and the big stewing pot was on the stove. All the things Mr. Kranky had bought were lined up near the sink.

"Come along, my boy!" cried Mr. Killy Kranky. "Which one did you put in first?"

"This one," George said. "Goldengloss Hair Shampoo." He emptied the bottle into the pot.

"Now the toothpaste," George went on. . . . "And the shaving soap . . . and the face cream . . . and the nail polish . . ."

"Keep at it, my boy!" cried Mr. Kranky, dancing around the kitchen. "Keep putting them in! Don't stop! Don't pause! Don't hesitate! It's a pleasure, my dear fellow, to watch you work!"

One by one, George poured and squeezed the things into the stewing pot. With everything so close at hand, the whole job didn't take him more than ten minutes. But when it was all done, the pot didn't somehow seem to be quite as full as it had been the first time.

"*Now* what did you do?" cried Mr. Kranky. "Did you stir it?"

"I boiled it," George said. "But not for long. And I stirred it as well."

So Mr. Kranky lit the gas under the pot and George stirred the mixture with the same long wooden spoon he had used before. "It's not brown enough," George said. "Wait a minute! I know what I've forgotten!"

"What?" cried Mr. Kranky. "Tell me, quick! Because if we've forgotten even one tiny thing, then it won't work! At least not in the same way."

"A quart of brown gloss paint," George said. "That's what I've forgotten."

Mr. Killy Kranky shot out of the house and into his car like a rocket. He sped down to the village and bought the paint and rushed back again. He opened the can in the kitchen and handed it to George. George poured the paint into the stewing pot.

"Ah-ha! That's better," George said. "That's more like the right color."

"It's boiling!" cried Mr. Kranky. "It's boiling and bubbling, George! Is it ready yet?"

"It's ready," George said. "At least I hope it is."

"Right!" shouted Mr. Kranky, hopping about. "Let's test it! Let's give some to a chicken!"

"My heavens alive, why don't you calm down a bit?" Mrs. Kranky said, coming into the kitchen.

"Calm down?" cried Mr. Kranky. "You expect me to *calm down* and here we are mixing up the greatest medicine ever discovered in the history of the world! Come along, George! Dip a cupful out of the pot and get a spoon and we'll give some to a chicken just to make absolutely certain we've got the correct mixture."

Outside in the yard, there were several chickens that hadn't had any of George's Marvelous Medicine Number One. They were pecking about in the dirt in that silly way chickens do.

George crouched down, holding out a spoonful of Marvelous Medicine Number Two. "Come on, chicken," he said. "Good chicken. Chick-chick-chick."

A white chicken with black specks on its feathers looked up at George. It walked over to the spoon and went *peck*.

The effect that Medicine Number Two had on this chicken was not quite the same as the effect produced by Medicine Number One, but it was very interesting. *"Whooosh!"* shrieked the chicken and it shot six feet up in the air and came down again. Then *sparks* came flying out of its beak, bright yellow sparks of fire, as though someone was sharpening a knife on a grindstone inside its tummy. Then its legs began to grow longer. Its body stayed the same size, but the two thin yellow legs got longer and longer and longer . . . and longer still. . . .

"What's happening to it?" cried Mr. Killy Kranky.

"Something's wrong," George said.

The legs went on growing and the more they grew, the higher up into the air went the chicken's body. When the legs were about fifteen feet long, they stopped growing. The chicken looked perfectly absurd with its long long legs and its ordinary little body perched high up on top. It was like a chicken on stilts.

"Oh my sainted aunts!" cried Mr. Killy Kranky. "We've got it wrong! This chicken's no good to anybody! It's all legs! No one wants chicken legs!"

"I must have left something out," George said.

"I *know* you left something out!" cried Mr. Kranky. "Think, boy, think! What was it you left out?"

"I've got it!" said George.

"What was it, quick?"

"Flea powder for dogs," George said.

"You mean you put *flea* powder in the first one?"

"Yes, Dad, I did. A whole carton of it."

"Then that's the answer!"

"Wait a minute," said George. "Did we have brown shoe polish on our list?"

"We did not," said Mr. Kranky.

"I used that, too," said George.

"Well, no *wonder* it went wrong," said Mr. Kranky. He was already running to his car, and soon he was heading down to the village to buy more flea powder and more shoe polish.

Marvelous Medicine Number Three

"**H**ere it is!" cried Mr. Killy Kranky, rushing into the kitchen. "One carton of flea powder for dogs and one can of brown shoe polish!"

George poured the flea powder into the giant stewing pot. Then he scooped the shoe polish out of its can and added that as well.

"Stir it up, George!" shouted Mr. Kranky. "Give it another boil! We've got it this time! I'll bet we've got it!"

After Marvelous Medicine Number Three had been boiled and stirred, George took a cupful of it out into the yard to try it on another chicken. Mr. Kranky ran after him, flapping his arms and hopping with excitement. "Come and watch this one!" he called out to Mrs. Kranky. "Come and watch us turning an ordinary chicken into a lovely great big one that lays eggs as large as footballs!"

"I hope you do better than last time," said Mrs. Kranky, following them out.

"Come on, chicken," said George, holding out a spoonful of Medicine Number Three. "Good chicken. Chick-chick-chick-chick-chick. Have some of this lovely medicine."

A magnificent black cockerel with a scarlet comb came stepping over. The cockerel looked at the spoon and it went *peck*.

"*Cock-a-doodle-do!*" squawked the cockerel, shooting up into the air and coming down again.

"Watch him now!" cried Mr. Kranky. "Watch him grow! Any moment he's going to start getting bigger and bigger!"

Mr. Killy Kranky, Mrs. Kranky and little George stood in the yard staring at the black cockerel. The cockerel stood quite still. It looked as though it had a headache.

"What's happening to its neck?" Mrs. Kranky said.

"It's getting longer," George said.

"I'll say it's getting longer," Mrs. Kranky said.

Mr. Kranky, for once, said nothing.

"Last time it was the legs," Mrs. Kranky said. "Now it's the neck. Who wants a chicken with a long neck? You can't eat a chicken's neck."

It was an extraordinary sight. The cockerel's body hadn't grown at all. But the neck was now about six feet long.

"All right, George," Mr. Kranky said. "What else have you forgotten?"

"I don't know," George said.

"Oh, yes you do," Mr. Kranky said. "Come on, boy, *think*. There's probably just one vital thing missing, and you've got to remember it."

"I put in some engine oil from the garage," George said. "Did you have that on your list?"

"Eureka!" cried Mr. Kranky. "That's the answer! How much did you put in?"

"Half a pint," George said.

Mr. Kranky ran to the garage and found another half pint of oil. "And some antifreeze," George called after him. "I sloshed in a bit of antifreeze."

Marvelous Medicine Number Four

Back in the kitchen once again, George, with Mr. Kranky watching him anxiously, tipped half a pint of engine oil and some antifreeze into the giant stewing pot.

"Boil it up again!" cried Mr. Kranky. "Boil it and stir it!"

George boiled it and stirred it.

"You'll never get it right," said Mrs. Kranky. "Don't forget you don't just have to have the same things but you've got to have exactly the same *amounts* of those things. And how can you possibly do that?"

"You keep out of this!" cried Mr. Kranky. "We're doing fine! We've got it this time, you see if we haven't!"

This was George's Marvelous Medicine Number Four, and when it had boiled for a couple of minutes, George once again carried a cupful of it out into the yard. Mr. Kranky ran after him. Mrs. Kranky followed more slowly. "You're going to have some mighty queer chickens around here if you go on like this," she said.

"Dish it out, George!" cried Mr. Kranky. "Give a spoonful to that one over there!" He pointed to a brown hen.

George knelt down and held out the spoon with the new medicine in it. "Chick-chick," he said. "Try some of this."

The brown hen walked over and looked at the spoon. Then it went *peck*.

"*Ouch!*" it said. Then a funny whistling noise came out of its beak.

"Watch it grow!" shouted Mr. Kranky.

"Don't be too sure," said Mrs. Kranky. "Why is it whistling like that?"

"Keep quiet, woman!" cried Mr. Kranky. "Give it a chance!"

They stood there staring at the brown hen.

"It's getting smaller," George said. "Look at it, Dad. It's shrinking."

And indeed it was. In less than a minute, the hen had shrunk so much it was no bigger than a new-hatched chick. It looked ridiculous.

Goodbye, Grandma

"There's still something you've left out," Mr. Kranky said.

"I can't think what it could be," George said.

"Give it up," Mrs. Kranky said. "Pack it in. You'll never get it right."

Mr. Kranky looked very forlorn.

George looked pretty fed up, too. He was still kneeling on the ground with the spoon in one hand and the cup full of medicine in the other. The ridiculous tiny brown hen was walking slowly away.

At that point, Grandma came striding into the yard. From her enormous height, she glared down at the three people below her and shouted, "What's going on around here? Why hasn't anyone brought me my morning cup of tea? It's bad enough having to sleep in the yard with the rats and mice, but I'll be blowed if I'm going to starve as well! No tea! No eggs and bacon! No buttered toast!"

"I'm sorry, Mother," Mrs. Kranky said. "We've been terribly busy. I'll get you something right away."

"Let George get it, the lazy little brute!" Grandma shouted.

Just then, the old woman spotted the cup in George's hand. She bent down and peered into it. She saw that it was full of brown liquid. It looked very much like tea. "Ho-ho!" she cried. "Ha-ha! So that's your little game, is it! You look after yourself all right, don't

78

you! You make quite sure *you've* got a nice cup of
morning tea! But you didn't think to bring one to your
poor old grandma! I always knew you were a selfish
pig!"

"No, Grandma," George said. "This isn't . . ."

"Don't lie to me, boy!" the enormous old hag shouted. "Pass it up here this minute!"

"No!" cried Mrs. Kranky. "No, Mother, don't! That's not for you!"

"Now *you're* against me, too!" shouted Grandma. "My own daughter trying to stop me having my breakfast! Trying to starve me out!"

Mr. Kranky looked up at the horrid old woman and smiled sweetly. "Of course it's for you, Grandma," he said. "You take it and drink it while it's nice and hot."

"Don't think I won't," Grandma said, bending down from her great height and reaching out a huge horny hand for the cup. "Hand it over, George."

"No, no Grandma!" George cried out, pulling the cup away. "You mustn't! You're not to have it!"

"Give it to me, boy!" yelled Grandma.

"Don't!" cried Mrs. Kranky. "That's George's Marvelous . . ."

"Everything's George's around here!" shouted Grandma. "George's this, George's that! I'm fed up with it!" She snatched the cup out of little George's hand and carried it high up out of reach.

"Drink it up, Grandma," Mr. Kranky said, grinning hugely. "Lovely tea."

"No!" the other two cried. "No, no, no!"

But it was too late. The ancient beanpole had already put the cup to her lips and in one gulp she swallowed everything that was in it.

"Mother!" wailed Mrs. Kranky. "You've just drunk fifty doses of George's Marvelous Medicine Number

Four, and look what one tiny spoonful did to that little old brown hen!"

But Grandma didn't even hear her. Great clouds of steam were already pouring out of her mouth and she was beginning to whistle.

81

"This is going to be interesting," Mr. Kranky said, still grinning.

"Now you've done it!" cried Mrs. Kranky, glaring at her husband. "You've cooked the old girl's goose!"

"I didn't do anything," Mr. Kranky said.

"Oh, yes you did! You told her to drink it!"

A tremendous hissing sound was coming from above their heads. Steam was shooting out of Grandma's mouth and nose and ears and whistling as it came.

"She'll feel better after she's let off a bit of steam," Mr. Kranky said.

"She's going to blow up!" Mrs. Kranky wailed.

"Her boiler's going to burst!"

"Stand clear," Mr. Kranky said.

George was quite alarmed. He stood up and ran back a few paces. The jets of white steam kept squirting out of the skinny old hag's head, and the whistling was so high and shrill it hurt the ears.

"Call the fire department!" cried Mrs. Kranky. "Call the police! Man the hoses!"

"Too late," said Mr. Kranky, looking pleased.

"Grandma!" shrieked Mrs. Kranky. "Mother! Run to the drinking trough and put your head under the water!"

But even as she spoke, the whistling suddenly stopped and the steam disappeared. That was when Grandma began to get smaller. She had started off with her head as high as the roof of the house, but now she was coming down fast.

"Watch this, George!" Mr. Kranky shouted, hopping around the yard and flapping his arms. "Watch what happens when someone's had fifty spoonfuls instead of one!"

Very soon, Grandma was back to normal height.

"Stop!" cried Mrs. Kranky. "That's just right."

But she didn't stop. Smaller and smaller she got . . . down and down she went. In another half minute she was no bigger than a bottle of lemonade.

"How d'you feel, Mother?" asked Mrs. Kranky anxiously.

Grandma's tiny face still bore the same foul and furious expression it had always had. Her eyes, no bigger now than little keyholes, were blazing with anger. "How do I *feel?*" she yelled. "How d'you *think* I feel? How would *you* feel if you'd been a glorious giant a minute ago and suddenly you're a miserable midget?"

"She's still going!" shouted Mr. Kranky gleefully. "She's still getting smaller!"

And by golly, she was.

When she was no bigger than a cigarette, Mrs. Kranky made a grab for her. She held her in her hands and cried, "How do I stop her getting smaller still?"

"You can't," said Mr. Kranky. "She's had fifty times the right amount."

"I *must* stop her!" Mrs. Kranky wailed. "I can hardly see her as it is!"

"Catch hold of each end and pull," Mr. Kranky said.

By then, Grandma was the size of a matchstick and still shrinking fast.

A moment later, she was no bigger than a pin. . . .

Then a pumpkin seed . . .

Then . . .

Then . . .

"Where is she?" cried Mrs. Kranky. "I've lost her!"

"Hooray," said Mr. Kranky.

"She's gone! She's disappeared completely!" cried Mrs. Kranky.

"That's what happens to you if you're grumpy and bad-tempered," said Mr. Kranky. "Great medicine of yours, George."

George didn't know what to think.

For a few minutes, Mrs. Kranky kept wandering around with a puzzled look on her face, saying, "Mother, where are you? Where've you gone? Where've you got to? How can I find you?" But she calmed down quite quickly. And by lunchtime, she was saying, "Ah well, I suppose it's all for the best, really. She was a bit of a nuisance around the house, wasn't she?"

"Yes," Mr. Kranky said. "She most certainly was."

George didn't say a word. He felt quite trembly. He knew something tremendous had taken place that morning. For a few brief moments he had touched with the very tips of his fingers the edge of a magic world.

TURN THE PAGE FOR A LOOK AT ANOTHER SCRUMDIDDLYUMPTIOUS STORY FROM ROALD DAHL!

Hairy Faces

What a lot of hairy-faced men there are around nowadays.

When a man grows hair all over his face it is impossible to tell what he really looks like.

Perhaps that's why he does it. He'd rather you didn't know.

Then there's the problem of washing.

When the very hairy ones wash their faces, it must be as big a job as when you and I wash the hair on our heads.

So what I want to know is this. How often do all these hairy-faced men wash their faces? Is it only once a week, like us, on Sunday nights? And do they shampoo it? Do they use a hairdryer? Do they rub hair tonic in to stop their faces from going bald? Do they go to a barber to have their hairy faces cut and trimmed or do they do it themselves in front of the bathroom mirror with nail scissors?

I don't know. But next time you see a man with a hairy face (which will probably be as soon as you step out onto the street) maybe you will look at him more closely and start wondering about some of these things.

Mr. Twit

Mr. Twit was one of these very hairy-faced men. The whole of his face except for his forehead, his eyes and his nose, was covered with thick hair. The stuff even sprouted in revolting tufts out of his nostrils and ear-holes.

Mr. Twit felt that this hairiness made him look terrifically wise and grand. But in truth he was neither of these things. Mr. Twit was a twit. He was born a twit. And now at the age of sixty, he was a bigger twit than ever.

The hair on Mr. Twit's face didn't grow smooth and matted as it does on most hairy-faced men. It grew in spikes that stuck out straight like the bristles of a nailbrush.

And how often did Mr. Twit wash this bristly nailbrushy face of his?

The answer is NEVER, not even on Sundays.

He hadn't washed it for years.

Dirty Beards

As you know, an ordinary unhairy face like yours or mine simply gets a bit smudgy if it is not washed often enough, and there's nothing so awful about that.

But a hairy face is a very different matter. Things *cling* to hairs, especially food. Things like gravy go right in among the hairs and stay there. You and I can wipe our smooth faces with a washcloth and we quickly look more or less all right again, but the hairy man cannot do that.

We can also, if we are careful, eat our meals without spreading food all over our faces. But not so the hairy man. Watch carefully next time you see a hairy man eating his lunch and you will notice that even if he opens his mouth very wide, it is impossible for him to get a spoonful of beef stew or ice cream and chocolate sauce into it without leaving some of it on the hairs.

Mr. Twit didn't even bother to open his mouth wide when he ate. As a result (and because he never washed) there were always hundreds of bits of old breakfasts and lunches and suppers sticking to the hairs around his face. They weren't big bits, mind you, because he used to wipe those off with the back of his hand or on his sleeve while he was eating. But if you looked closely (not that you'd ever want to) you would see tiny little specks of dried-up scrambled eggs stuck to the hairs, and spinach and tomato ketchup and fishsticks and minced chicken livers and all the other disgusting things Mr. Twit liked to eat.

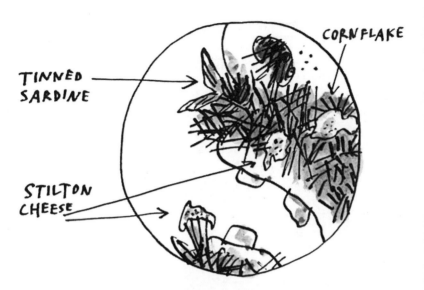

CORNFLAKE

TINNED
SARDINE

STILTON
CHEESE

If you looked closer still (hold your noses, ladies and gentlemen), if you peered deep into the moustachy bristles sticking out over his upper lip, you would probably see much larger objects that had escaped the wipe of his hand, things that had been there for months and months, like a piece of maggoty green cheese or a moldy old cornflake or even the slimy tail of a tinned sardine.

Because of all this, Mr. Twit never went really hungry. By sticking out his tongue and curling it sideways to explore the hairy jungle around his mouth, he was always able to find a tasty morsel here and there to nibble on.

What I am trying to tell you is that Mr. Twit was a foul and smelly old man.

He was also an extremely horrid old man as you will find out in a moment.

Mrs. Twit

Mrs. Twit was no better than her husband.

She did not, of course, have a hairy face. It was a pity she didn't because that, at any rate, would have hidden some of her fearful ugliness.

Take a look at her.

Have you ever seen a woman with an uglier face than that? I doubt it.

But the funny thing is that Mrs. Twit wasn't born ugly. She'd had quite a nice face when she was young. The ugliness had grown upon her year by year as she got older.

Why would that happen? I'll tell you why.

If a person has ugly thoughts, it begins to show on the face. And when that person has ugly thoughts every day, every week, every year, the face gets uglier and uglier until it gets so ugly you can hardly bear to look at it.

A person who has good thoughts cannot ever be ugly. You can have a wonky nose and a crooked mouth and a double chin and stick-out teeth, but if you have good thoughts they will shine out of your face like sunbeams and you will always look lovely.

Nothing good shone out of Mrs. Twit's face.

In her right hand she carried a walking stick. She used to tell people that this was because she had warts growing on the sole of her left foot and walking was painful. But the real reason she carried a stick was so that she could hit things with it, things like dogs and cats and small children.

And then there was the glass eye. Mrs. Twit had a glass eye that was always looking the other way.

The Glass Eye

You can play a lot of tricks with a glass eye because you can take it out and pop it back in again any time you like. You can bet your life Mrs. Twit knew all the tricks.

One morning she took out her glass eye and dropped it into Mr. Twit's mug of beer when he wasn't looking.

Mr. Twit sat there drinking the beer slowly. The froth made a white ring on the hairs around his mouth. He wiped the white froth on to his sleeve and wiped his sleeve on his trousers.

"You're plotting something," Mrs. Twit said, keeping her back turned so he wouldn't see that she had taken out her glass eye. "Whenever you go all quiet like that I know very well you're plotting something."

Mrs. Twit was right. Mr. Twit was plotting away like mad. He was trying to think up a really nasty trick he could play on his wife that day.

"You'd better be careful," Mrs. Twit said, "because when I see you starting to plot, I watch you like a wombat."

"Oh, do shut up, you old hag," Mr. Twit said. He went on drinking his beer, and his evil mind kept working away on the latest horrid trick he was going to play on the old woman.

Suddenly, as Mr. Twit tipped the last drop of beer down his throat, he caught sight of Mrs. Twit's awful glass eye staring up at him from the bottom of the mug. It made him jump.

"I told you I was watching you," cackled Mrs. Twit. "I've got eyes everywhere so you'd better be careful."

The Frog

To pay her back for the glass eye in his beer, Mr. Twit decided he would put a frog in Mrs. Twit's bed.

He caught a big one down by the pond and carried it back secretly in a box.

That night, when Mrs. Twit was in the bathroom getting ready for bed, Mr. Twit slipped the frog between her sheets. Then he got into his own bed and waited for the fun to begin.

Mrs. Twit came back and climbed into her bed and put out the light. She lay there in the dark scratching her tummy. Her tummy was itching. Dirty old hags like her always have itchy tummies.

Then all at once she felt something cold and slimy crawling over her feet. She screamed.

"What's the matter with you?" Mr. Twit said.

"Help!" screamed Mrs. Twit, bouncing about. "There's something in my bed!"

"I'll bet it's that Giant Skillywiggler I saw on the floor just now," Mr. Twit said.

"That *what?*" screamed Mrs. Twit.

"I tried to kill it but it got away," Mr. Twit said. "It's got teeth like screwdrivers!"

"Help!" screamed Mrs. Twit. "Save me! It's all over my feet!"

"It'll bite off your toes," said Mr. Twit.

Mrs. Twit fainted.

Mr. Twit got out of bed and fetched a jug of cold water. He poured the water over Mrs. Twit's head to revive her. The frog crawled up from under the sheets to get near the water. It started jumping about on the pillow. Frogs love water. This one was having a good time.

When Mrs. Twit came to, the frog had just jumped onto her face. This is not a nice thing to happen to anyone in bed at night. She screamed again.